# Bones
## of the
# Voyager

Written by
## Lynn Almengor

Illustrated by
## Janet Figueroa

Plaid Core Productions
PHILADELPHIA, PA

## Content Notice

This story is about depression. It talks about suicide, but doesn't depict or idealize it. If you're experiencing a crisis or otherwise need someone to talk to, please call the 988 Suicide & Crisis Lifeline at 988 or 1.800.273.8255.

No animals are harmed in this story.

## Copyright 2025 by Lynn Almengor / Plaid Core Productions

## Publisher's Cataloging-in-Publication Data

Names: Lynn Almengor, author ; Janet Figueroa, illustrator.
Title: Bones of the Voyager.
Edition: 1st.
Description: Philadelphia, PA : Plaid Core Productions, 2025.
Identifiers: ISBN 978-0-9974208-3-8 (pbk.) | LCCN 2025911027.
Physical description: 164 pages ; illustrations ; 12 cm.
Subjects: LCSH Depression, Mental--FICTION. | Independent films--FICTION. | Community theater--FICTION. | Voyager Project--FICTION. | Existential psychology--FICTION. | Philadelphia (Pa.)-- FICTION. | BISAC COMICS & GRAPHIC NOVELS / Literary | COMICS & GRAPHIC NOVELS / Contemporary Women | COMICS & GRAPHIC NOVELS / Disability.

For my sister Laura, who's been by my side through it all,
literally for as long as I can remember.

–Lynn

Para mi madre Bertha, who never gave up on me,
despite my diagnosis of Autism. She made sure I got
a good education and helped me learn to talk, read,
and write in a language she barely understands.
Gracias Mama. Te amo con todo mi corazon.

–Janet

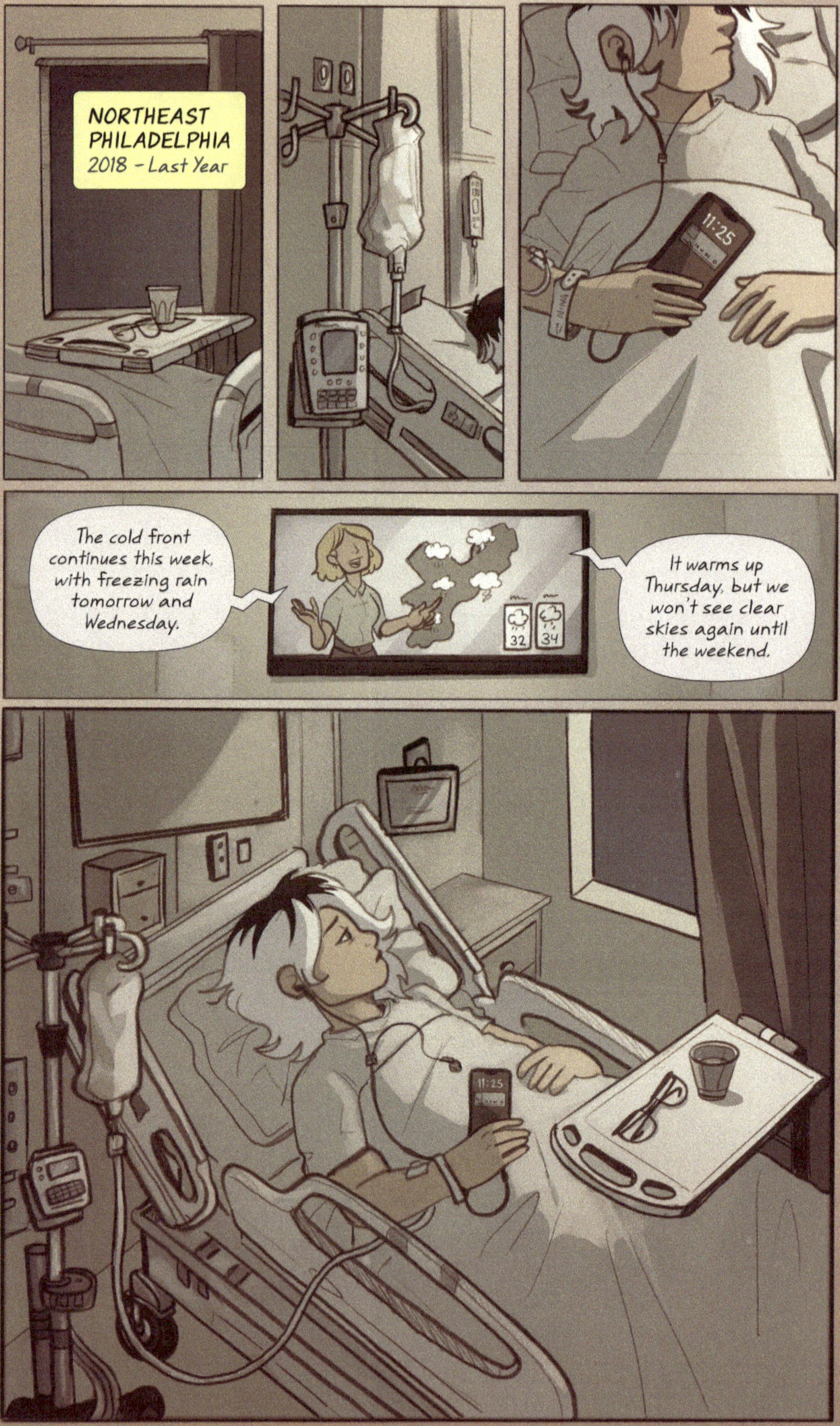

NORTHEAST
PHILADELPHIA
2018 – Last Year

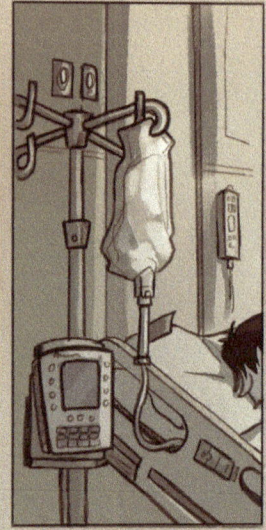

The cold front continues this week, with freezing rain tomorrow and Wednesday.

It warms up Thursday, but we won't see clear skies again until the weekend.

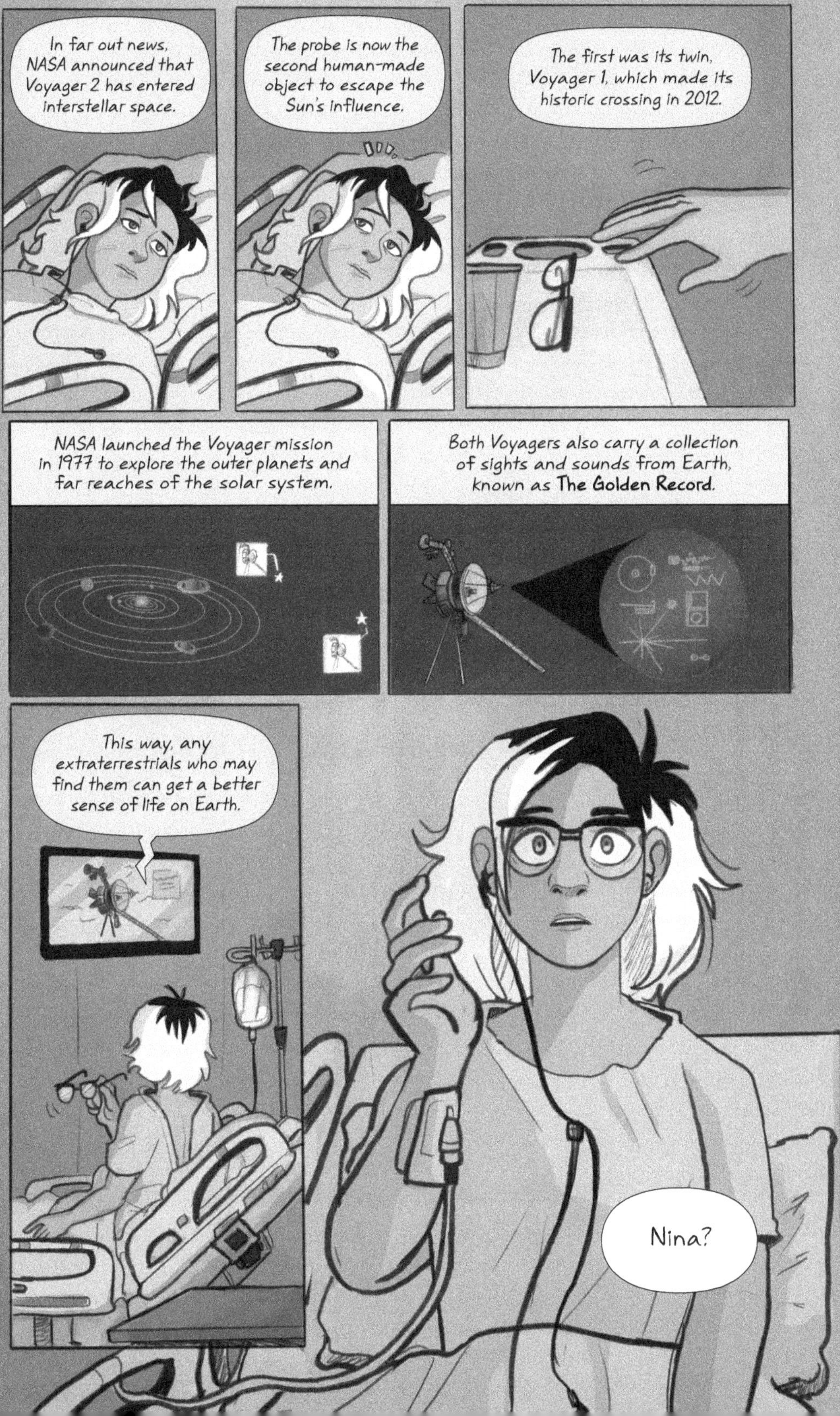

In far out news, NASA announced that Voyager 2 has entered interstellar space.

The probe is now the second human-made object to escape the Sun's influence.

The first was its twin, Voyager 1, which made its historic crossing in 2012.

NASA launched the Voyager mission in 1977 to explore the outer planets and far reaches of the solar system.

Both Voyagers also carry a collection of sights and sounds from Earth, known as **The Golden Record.**

This way, any extraterrestrials who may find them can get a better sense of life on Earth.

Nina?

NINA!

I somehow got it down here without questions.

NORTHEAST PHILADELPHIA 2019 – Present Day

Hiya Gorgeous! Whaddya say you and me hit the town tonight?

No offense, but you're not my type.

Ya cut me to the core, doll!

You LITERALLY don't have a core.

Now yer just bein' mean.

6

How about "VINCENZO?"

In honor of all the pizza we're gonna eat this weekend.

He needs a name.

HOSPITAL

I love it!

Really?

What? He's a valued cast member.

I'm not rolling out the red carpet until he proves he can act.

Cass and Nina, sisters extraordinaire!

Take five, everyone!

You're not the director.

JOANNA IS NOT THE DIRECTOR!

Are these the costumes?

They **COULD** be...

...but if you really wanna capture people's imaginations, might I suggest...

TADA!

SHINY SPACE SUITS!

I need people to **IDENTIFY** with the characters, not be distracted by their fabulous costumes.

Your day will come.

10

This seems too big for Roman.

How much can you take something in before it looks silly?

We're dressing up as aliens. It's inherently silly.

Hey now. We agreed the retro explorer vibe was cool.

I'm not wearing that.

Stand down, **Edward Scissorhands.**

Nina insists her aliens be as boring as you.

You're making a movie about **ALIENS?!**

It's about alien bones connecting telepathically with people to get closure on their life.

Like if aliens were also ghosts.

That's so cool!

You know, some scientists say we haven't met aliens yet because civilizations always destroy themselves before they can perfect interstellar travel.

But I prefer to think Earth is in a rural dead zone.

Is that the guy who didn't get cast, but keeps showing up anyway?

Yup.

You wanna help with the film?

It's Wyatt again.

He wants to know if his wife can help too. Says she took film classes in college.

What are you saying?

Asking if she can do lighting.

You wanna bring on a lighting tech the day before we start shooting?

What if she's no good?

Anything's better than doing it myself.

13

Good night, Egg.

Good night, Bean.

14

I did stuff that mattered today.

But not EVERY day.

What percentage of your total days do you think were productive?

Hssss...

I don't have time for this.

It was YOUR bright idea to write a story about bones.

Go away, VINCENZO.

SOUTHERN
NEW MEXICO
1997 – 22 Years Ago

D-Dad?

Hey Beth. How's the song going?

I still don't feel any closer to the truth.

20

How was rehearsal?

Joanna's girlfriend's sister is making a movie about aliens.

She said I could help.

Rock on.

She said *YOU* could help too...

Wy...

I know. But you've been stuck on this song about your dad forever.

Maybe doing something else could help you get un-stuck.

That's very sweet, but I doubt it.

Shatter!!

Wyatt?

Are you okay?

Sorry, I broke a picture frame.

What are you doing?

The director asked if I could bring power strips and extension cords.

Said he couldn't be friends with Wyatt anymore because *I* would always be around.

Secretly moved out of the house while I was away.

Stopped speaking to us after I called her new boyfriend a "sexist shitbag."

Said I use my bipolar as an excuse to be an asshole.

Still loves me for some reason.

What's this film about?

Something about alien bones sending telepathic messages to the future.

That sounds terrible.

I think it sounds cool.

Fine, whatever. I'll do it.

Really?

Maybe you're right. Maybe I'll be inspired...

Since you're still here, I guess I have about two weeks before I'm full-on depressed.

Could be less.

You're supposed to give me until at least October. I planned my whole film around it.

You know what they say, "the best laid plans of ferrets and women..."

No one says that.

We might be able to cut the third weekend if we shoot a few extra scenes per day.

It's cute how you still think you can plan around me.

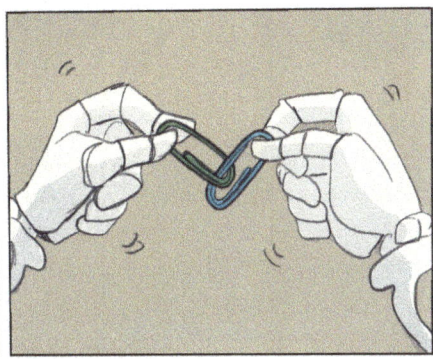

TWO HOURS LATER

10:55

Unknown #

This is Wyatt's wife, Beth. I have questions about the film. Can you call me?

You forgot to submit your work.

Oh well. If people knew how fast I am, they'd give me more work.

Then I wouldn't be able to keep up the pace when *YOU* show up.

Plus, if I only give 50% most days, then giving 75% during emergencies makes me seem like a team player.

You should write your next film about that.
Call it, *How to Be Average.*
I'M NOT **AVERAGE,** I'M **EFFICIENT!**
EXIT
It's not ***MY*** fault society forces artists to waste the better part of our lives earning the right to exist with meaningless day jobs.
Now you just sound pretentious.
AAAAAAAAH!!

Yo.

Hi, this is Nina, director of **Bones of the Voyager.**

Wyatt said you have lighting experience?

I *CAN* do lighting, but I'd rather do camerawork or set design.

I've got everything else covered.

What kind of lighting vibe are you going for?

BE Nice!!

Kinda dark, with the visions projected into people's minds looking more dreamlike.

Sure.

So you think you can do that?

What's your equipment situation?

I usually bounce garage lamps off the ceiling and hope for the best.

Oh, hell no.

If I'm lighting this thing, we're doing it right.

Thank you both for doing this so last minute!

We were free anyway.

I don't work weekends and Beth doesn't have a job.

Beth said you process mail for Admissions?

Yup! And employees can take classes and use the facilities for free.

I'll take a pack of colored gels too.

Nina's here!

What kind of camera do you have?

Panasonic DVX-100.

Are you shitting me? That thing's ancient.

I shot all my films with it.

Do they even **MAKE** Mini-DV tapes anymore?

Yup! I already blacked them.

Wow. Just... wow.

Okay, lighting's covered. You need mics?

We could probably use a better boom. Mine's as old as my camera.

What about lapel mics?

I still have a few things to do before the shoot.

Get whatever you want as long as you're cool with figuring out how it all works.

Thanks for taking this. Our car's pretty small.

No probz!

For a supposed filmmaker, you don't know jack about equipment.

I know how to frame a shot and tell a story.

Those kids know more about filmmaking than you ever will.

They're probably not even film majors.

When I was in college, there were no smartphones and social media was barely a thing.

Now every kid in America has their own video channel.

At this point, my only hope of standing out IS keeping it old school.

Cry me a river, Grandma.

You know none of this stuff works.

I only need to make it through shooting.

I've written and directed three films.

That makes me a filmmaker, even if my work never earns money or gets attention.

With every film, I moved past the stuff that was bothering me and learned something new about myself.

And no one can ever take that away from me. Not even *YOU*.

**TAKE. ME. TO. YOUR. LEAD-ER.**

And over here are my cosmic co-stars, putting the finishing touches on our costumes.

Please don't post that.

**STRIKE A POSE, ROMAN!**

We look like idiots.

Pfft. Party pooper.

You knew about the alien thing before you signed on.

I wasn't sure about the purple makeup, but somehow you made it look... classy?

Because I'm amazing, obviously.

≋Scoff≋

*I can't believe this is my life...

You okay?

I'm a little depressed, but I'll be fine.

We can always do this another time when you feel better.

But I never know how long it's gonna last.

If I waste a single moment of the time I can still function, it'll only make me more depressed.

Yo.

Where should we set up?

Thanks for checking on me, Cass.

But right now, we've got a film to make!

How's the sound?

You don't need me for this, right?

Nope. This is just a short scene with Cass to test the equipment.

How do you want the lights?

However you think is best. But be consistent.

Well, what's happening in this scene?

Didn't you read the script?

It's easier if you tell me what you want as we go.

And you thought you were playing on hard mode *BEFORE*.

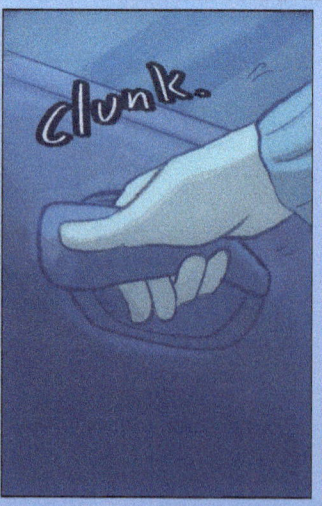

clunk.

Clunk!
clunk!

clunk!
clunk!

That was awesome!

Is that it for tonight?

Yup! Everything looks and sounds good!

Hell yeah! Can I say the thing?

Go for it!

THAT'S A WRAP!

Yay!

Tomorrow we'll meet at the hospital at 8am.

Then we'll head to my office, the park, and the road behind the farm.

When do we go to the bathroom?

We don't.

It's not as bad as it sounds.

But what's the rush? You have a deadline or something?

I shot my first film over six months, and it was a consistency nightmare.

The weather would change, people's hair would grow...

Plus, it's hard to take your character on an emotional journey when there's weeks between scenes.

Fair enough. But I can be an asshole when I'm tired.

Don't say I didn't warn you.

Don't worry. We'll have plenty of coffee and snacks to get us through!

Come on,
*Fall Out Boy.*
It's time.

48

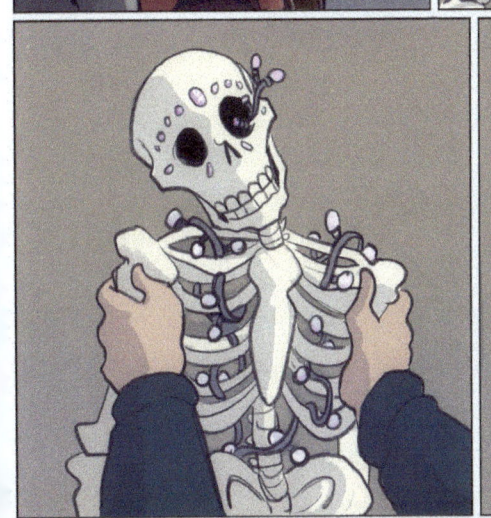

Jean Valjean?!

I thought you moved to New York.

I'm just back visiting family...

Things start getting weird in this scene.

Could you make the lighting feel off-kilter?

Roger.

Could you also work Vincenzo's lights? They're on a dimmer switch.

What the hell is happening in this scene?

Radiation from the scanner activates the bones.

Vincenzo obviously looks fake, so we'll only show his glowing outline under the sheet.

Why would you do a CAT scan on bones?

To analyze the internal structures without destroying them.

The machines used for that are more powerful than hospital scanners, but the principle is the same.

How would *YOU* know?

He has degrees in geology and astrobiology.

A—Alright. Geez.

First, we have to remove personal effects from the cubes.

Take photos so we remember where everything goes.

LUDA ZENO

Hey **Red!** We need more light out here.

I can't believe you brought the skull.

We might need it.

I found something!

Well?

There's not much. Only a few photos and a heavily redacted report.

Awesome! I think we're ready to move downstairs.

Wait. That's it? They waltz right in, get the info, and leave?

What do you mean?

Why would a facility housing alien bones give the janitor access to classified files?

It's not supposed to be a conspiracy thriller.

It's a portrait of three people facing the unknown.

It feels unrealistic.

Okay. Give me a minute to think.

Remember your crime scene where the cop didn't immediately check the body?

I did so much research on the **QUESTIONS** a cop might ask, I didn't realize my mistake until I overheard that couple at the premiere.

You felt pretty stupid.

To be fair, that scene was about the witness's reaction.

No one else ever mentioned it.

To your face.

What if Wyatt played a security guard?

Me?

You auditioned for Bensalem Players, right?

I'LL DO IT.

We have police costumes at the theatre, but it would take over an hour to get them.

It's September. I'm sure there's a pop-up Halloween store nearby.

Wyatt, Beth, and Joanna can go find a costume...

...while Cass, Roman, and I shoot the scene downstairs.

Hey Wyatt. Have you ever tried **box breathing?**

No...

Take a deep breath for 4 seconds.

Hold it for 4 seconds.

Exhale for 4 seconds.

Then hold it again for 4 seconds.

Repeat it as many times as you need to.

I had a panic attack at a Broadway audition.

At least if you mess up here, we can do another take.

Look what else I got at the store!

It's perfect for when we direct *The Toxic Avenger!*

Since when are we directing *The Toxic Avenger?*

Since **TODAY!**

Obviously, you'll also play Sara.

Like Bensalem Players would ever do that show.

Pshh. I can handle Bensalem Players.

How are you feeling?

I'm ready.

Let's run through the scene once or twice before we start recording.

That way we can both practice.

You rocked it, Wy!

I still have to do it for real, though...

Nope! I recorded the practice takes, just in case.

You're done!

Really?

The scene was better with you in it.

The added threat really keeps the energy up.

Alright! Costume change!

What's with having the same actors play the aliens?

Is it supposed to mean something?

It's to keep the cast small.

Ten years ago, people loved getting involved, but they're too busy now.

Most of our theatre friends don't act anymore.

I get that people have lives, but it's tough thinking smaller.

Screw 'em. They wanna be boring, let 'em.

Maybe they tried their best, but it didn't work out.

Meh.

I'll support anyone being creative, even if their show's terrible.

Alright, we're rolling, and—

Hold on.

How's the lighting now?

THUMP!

These shots need to be more dramatic.

That was so rad!

What if you got *IN* the water?

That's it. I'm out.

Just like that?

Either way, they're *DEAD.*

We don't know whether the bones belong to the victim or the murderer!

Death clearly isn't the same for them!

What if it's a trap?

The visions don't feel malicious. It has to be the woman. She must have something to say.

I can't turn back without knowing.

GAH! FINE!

But don't blame me when we all *DIE!*

Can I say the thing?

Absolutely!

THAT'S A WRAP!

If Cass was close enough to the bones to see that first vision...

...then technically, the guard should've seen the second one.

That's what you get for compromising your creative vision.

You're the one who said Beth's ideas were better!

You're the one who didn't think through the consequences.

Maybe only people around for the initial incident would be affected.

It's not like the film made sense to begin with.

SHUT UP, VINCENZO!

Why won't you direct with me? You're helping Nina...

First off, she asked.

And I'm not **DIRECTING**— only helping her with costumes and props.

I don't see the difference.

I love helping, but hate feeling **OBLIGATED.**

Especially when it's something I don't enjoy.

I got excited by the idea of working on a fun show together.

I didn't mean to upset you.

I'll still be your Sara and help with stuff.

But ask first, okay?

No problem, **froglem.**

I read the script last night.

And?

Nothing happens. They don't even find anything in the woods.

That's the point.

I don't get it.

Our lives are a random collection of events we force into context.

They don't **MEAN** anything.

Then you need to **SAY** that with your story.

83

FANTASTIC!

Joanna, can you talk to them? You speak Spanish.

Only enough to disappoint my family!

¡Muévete para allá!*

They'll be here for a few more hours.

Maybe this can still work...

No matter how far those kids go, the mic will still pick them up.

Technically, we only need this location for the end of the scene.

The rest could take place in any wooded area.

How about the woods behind the theatre?

*Move over there!

It should be right here.

This doesn't look like the place from the vision.

I feel something. It's this way.

All these woods shots are starting to look the same.

Please be careful!

THIS LOOKS AMAZING!

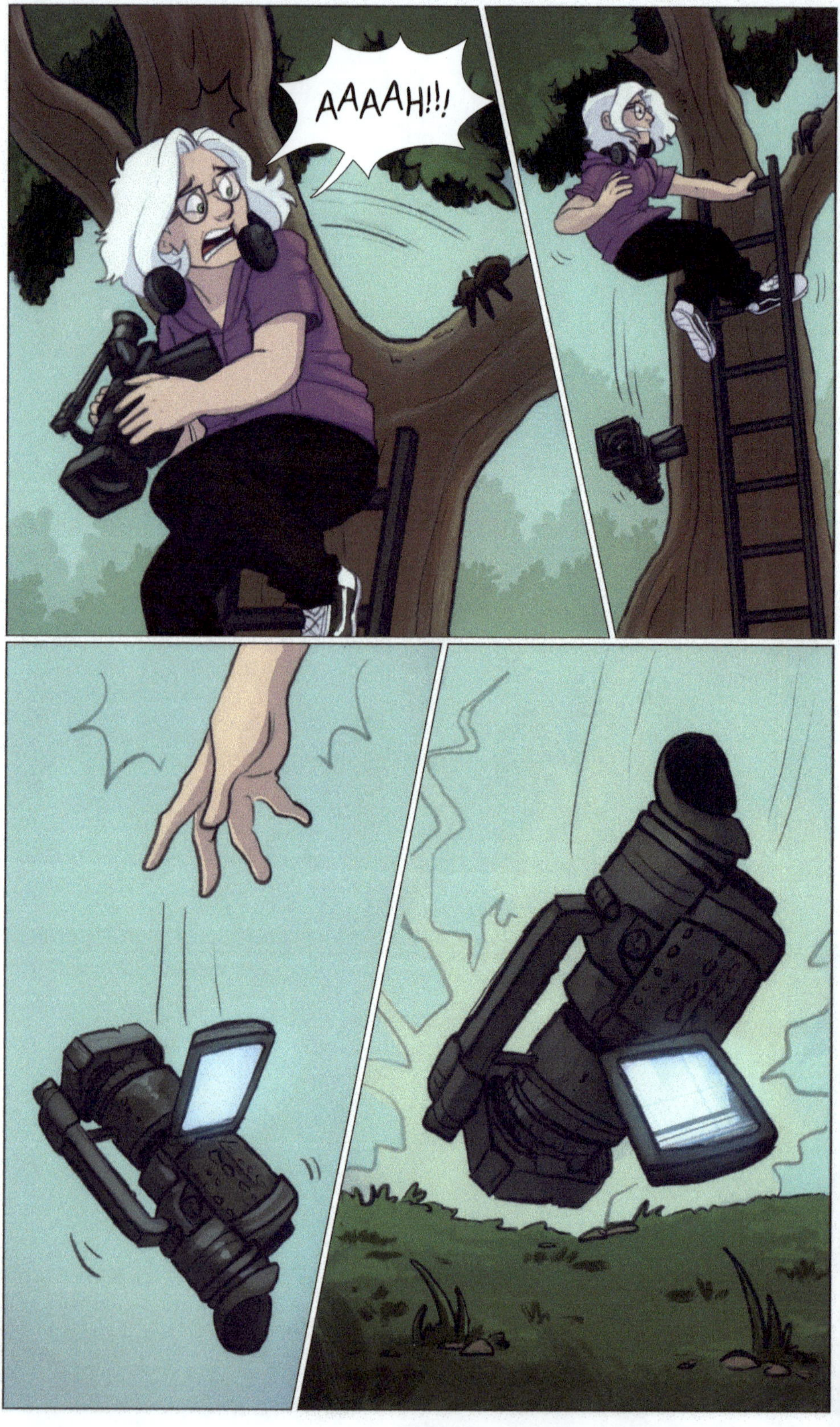
AAAAH!!!

What happened?!

THERE WAS A HUGE SPIDER!

Are you okay?!

Can you use the eyehole viewfinder instead?

I'll lose my peripheral vision.

Pack it up. We're done.

93

THREE WEEKS LATER

The OPENING NIGHT

Barefoot in the Park
Saturday 8pm
day 2pm

TICKETS

Two minutes, Wyatt.

Thank you, two minutes.

I blink the lights so people know it's time to start.

Break a leg, or whatever weird shit theatre people say these days.

Yo.

Big night for Wyatt.

He's having the time of his life.

How's Nina?

She goes to work, but shuts down at home.

How long has she had depression?

Since always. But a few years ago, it got much worse.

Ugh. Roman got cast as Captain Von Trapp at Mason's Mill, and won't shut up about it.

Is that prestigious or something?

They don't even have a cast bathroom!

They make us use a porta-toilet out back!

He's probably happy it's a role regular people know and respect.

He's kidding himself if he thinks Mason's Mill is better than Bensalem Players.

It's where we met, though.

That's the only good thing about it.

How did you two meet?

We worked at a video store.

I accidentally got her fired.

Some asshole insulted Wy's intelligence over a five-dollar DVD, so I tore him a new one.

Guy's friend recorded me on his phone and sent it to corporate.

That's terrible!

Whatever. They went bankrupt and I got to keep Wyatt.

I love you.

97

DING DONG!

DING-di-di-ding-ding-ding-DONG!!

Are you on meds?

They made me feel like I had dementia.

It was worse than being depressed.

I lost count of how many I tried before I found one that worked.

For three straight months last year, the only way I could feel anything was listening to ska.

But eventually, I came out the other side.

What if next time you don't?

I don't know, okay?

Everyone who gets to the breaking point first feels like you do now.

Meds, therapy... Try **SOMETHING** before it gets harder.

A therapist told me I was "too smart" to have my problems.

The one I went to after my dad died made fun of me for bringing a stuffed animal.

I was 14.

Was your dad bipolar too?

Most likely.

Right before he died, he bought a truck and took me on a cross-country road trip.

We got as far as New Mexico before he dropped into an intense depression.

I had to call my grandma from a pay phone to come get us.

I'm sorry.

I've been trying to write a song about it.

But I'm never sure whether I'm getting closer to the truth or simply filling in the gaps with my own experiences.

Sometimes I think I've already written the best thing I'll ever write.

What made you want to tell your story?

I've always been fascinated by astronomy.

I was in the hospital when Voyager 2 entered interstellar space.

The timing felt... **IMPORTANT** somehow.

I hoped it would all click at some point, but it clearly didn't.

Try not to be so hard on yourself.

What did you say the other day? That meaning only exists through context?

Sounds like something I'd say...

Maybe we haven't given our projects the right context yet.

Yo.

What if we went to that rest stop in New Mexico and finished the film as a music video for your song about your dad?

I... what?!

It might help you remember something.

That's absurd.

Is it?

How would that even work?

Your film has nothing to do with my song.

We take out the dialogue and change the visions to tell a father-daughter story.

What could I possibly learn from a parking lot and a couple of rest rooms?

It doesn't have to make sense to be worth it.

Once again, you're diving headfirst into a half-baked project in a desperate attempt to fill the void.

Is this helping you at all?

Maybe?

I'm not doing this unless you really want to.

How can I give it my all when we don't even know if everyone's on board?

Okay. I'll call Roman, you call Wyatt.

Right now?!

121

Well, that's the plan. What do you think?

You had me at Roswell.

Sounds fun!

Hell yeah, **ROAD TRIP!**

I don't know...

What about you, *Edgar Allen Roe?*

It won't be the same without you.

After this, it's really over?

I promise! Next time I call you, it'll be for something else entirely.

Well, if you insist...

*YAY!*

**A FEW WEEKS LATER**

I love you both so much! Be good for Grandma and Grandpa, okay?

And thank you, Egg. For everything.

You ready?

Nope.

We got you, fam.

Come on, everyone!

**TEAM ALIEN!**

124

TEMP 58. 12:43 P.M

We mostly drove until something caught his eye.

What kind of things did you do on the trip with your dad?

He'd make a big deal about all this mundane shit, and I never bothered to ask him about it.

I'd roll my eyes and go back to thinking about something equally inconsequential.

All kids do that.

I couldn't understand my parents until I watched them interact with the world as a fellow adult.

I'm sorry you didn't get a chance to do that.

I know I couldn't have stopped him.

But that doesn't make me feel better.

*Of all the damned times!

129

Did you ever consider moving to New York or LA?

Not really.

Why not? You're actually good at this.

Philly's my home.

When I lived in New York, I went to 82 auditions.

I got called back 6 times.

No one ever cast me.

It's awful when you can't do the thing you love without permission.

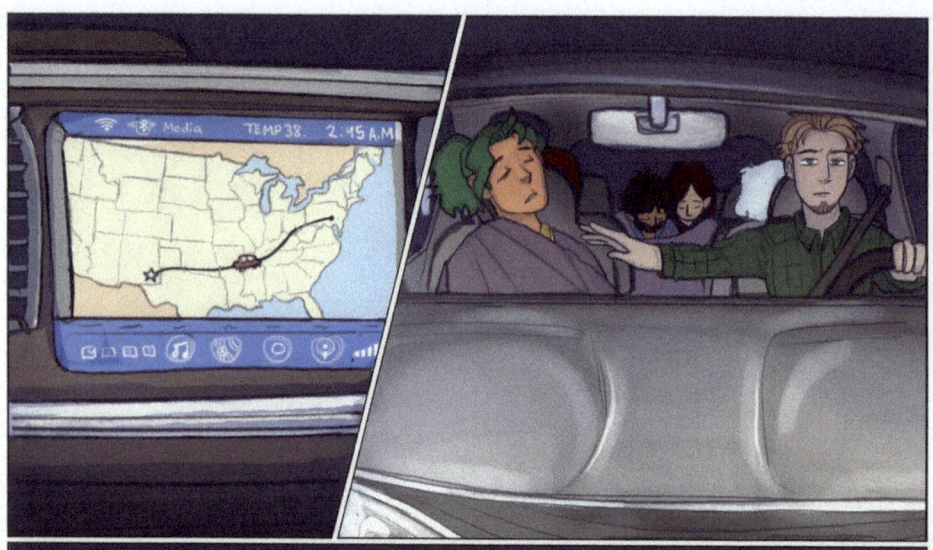

Hey... I know you didn't care about the film. But you took it seriously because you care about **ME**.

Thank you for that.

I cared about the film.

Seriously. You're so kind to everyone. I'm sorry I didn't do enough for you.

What are you talking about?

I should've defended you more to Mom and Dad and the kids at school.

But instead, I told you not to fight back, because it would make things worse.

I don't remember you saying that.

So it clearly didn't scar me for life the way your space facts did.

I'm still sorry.

You weren't usually the one upsetting me.

You laughed at my stupid jokes and played **Bubble Bobble** with me when I had a bad day.

Were **Bub** and **Bob** aliens?

I don't think so. They got transformed back into humans in the good ending.

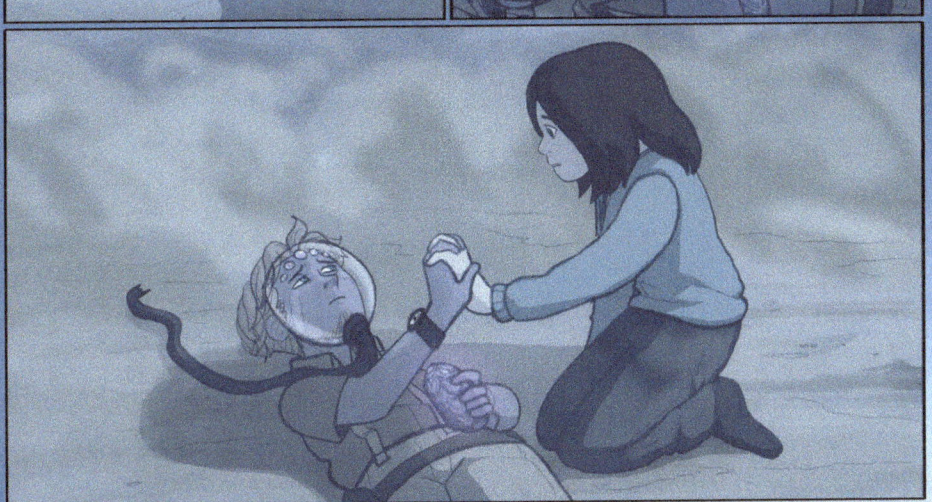

CUT!

THIS IS **BULLSHIT!**

**WE WEREN'T ALIENS!**

I GOT SWEPT UP IN YOUR GRANDIOSITY, BUT NONE OF THIS WAS EVER ABOUT **ME**.

IT WAS ABOUT USING MY PAIN TO SALVAGE YOUR PATHETIC EXCUSE FOR A FILM.

I didn't get to say goodbye...

FUCK YOU.

You can have your story back.
Someday, you'll figure out what it means.

You gotta say the thing.

Seriously? We didn't finish the film.

Come on, don't be a Roman.

As if.

Fine, whatever.

That's a wrap.